TUBBY the TUBA

Paul Tripp
illustrated by Henry Cole

Dutton Children's Books

For Ruth—always—
—P. T.

For Michael and Daniel, wonderful neighbors, wonderful friends
And special thanks to the fabulous Heather Wood
—H. C.

Dutton Children's Books
A DIVISION OF PENGUIN YOUNG READERS GROUP

PUBLISHED BY THE PENGUIN GROUP Penguin Group (USA) Inc., 375 Hudson Street, New York, New York 10014, U.S.A. / Penguin Group (Canada), 90 Eglinton Avenue East, Suite 700, Toronto, Ontario, Canada M4P 2Y3 (a division of Pearson Penguin Canada Inc.) / Penguin Books Ltd, 80 Strand, London WC2R 0RL, England / Penguin Ireland, 25 St Stephen's Green, Dublin 2, Ireland (a division of Penguin Books Ltd) / Penguin Group (Australia), 250 Camberwell Road, Camberwell, Victoria 3124, Australia (a division of Pearson Australia Group Pty Ltd) / Penguin Books India Pvt Ltd, 11 Community Centre, Panchsheel Park, New Delhi - 110 017, India / Penguin Group (NZ), Cnr Airborne and Rosedale Roads, Albany, Auckland 1310, New Zealand (a division of Pearson New Zealand Ltd) / Penguin Books (South Africa) (Pty) Ltd, 24 Sturdee Avenue, Rosebank, Johannesburg 2196, South Africa / Penguin Books Ltd, Registered Offices: 80 Strand, London WC2R 0RL, England

Library of Congress Cataloging-in-Publication Data
Tripp, Paul.
Tubby the Tuba / by Paul Tripp; illustrated by Henry Cole.—1st ed.
p. cm.
Summary: With some help from a frog, Tubby the Tuba shows the orchestra that tubas can play melodies as well as other instruments. ISBN 978-0-525-47717-4
[1. Tuba—Fiction. 2. Musical instruments—Fiction. 3. Frogs—Fiction. 4. Orchestra—Fiction.] I. Cole, Henry, 1955– ill. II. Title.
PZ7.T736Tu 2006 [E]—dc22 2005035035

Published in the United States by Dutton Children's Books,
a division of Penguin Young Readers Group, 345 Hudson Street, New York, New York 10014
www.penguin.com/youngreaders

Designed by Heather Wood / Manufactured in China
First Edition 10 9 8 7 6 5 4 3

Once upon a time, there was an orchestra, which was all busy tuning up.

First, the oboe gave his A note to the strings, to the woodwinds, and to the brass.

Up and around the scales they raced,
helter-skelter,
faster and faster—

all but Tubby the Tuba, a fat little tuba, puffing away, but

oh

so

slow.

Oh, what lovely music,
thought Tubby, and sighed.

"Here! What's the matter?" said Peepo the Piccolo.

"Oh," said Tubby, "every time we do a new piece, you all get such pretty melodies to play, and I . . . never, never a pretty melody."

"But," said Peepo, "people never write melodies for tubas. It just isn't done!"

"Oh, there's the conductor. *Shhhhhh.*"

The conductor rapped his baton. Then the instruments began to play.
First, the violins danced a lovely little tune on their strings.
Then they cried to the flute, "Catch!"
"Got it," cried the flute.
"My turn," tooted the trumpet.
And the rest joined in. The cello. The oboe.
The bassoon.

While Tubby went *oompah, oompah.*
"Catch me!" cried the little tune.
"Catch me!"
"Got you!" cried Tubby.

"Oh, you're sitting on me," said the little tune.
Poor Tubby picked up the flat little tune and
tried to squeeze it back into shape.

"Oh, you clumsy fool," snapped the violins.
"I'm sorry, Mister Fiddle," said Tubby.

"Fiddle, well!" And the violins quivered with great indignation.
"You will please address us as violins! Fiddles, indeed!"

"Tubby," said the conductor. "Tubby, what is the matter?"

"Please, sir, I thought it would be so nice to dance with the pretty little tune, instead of going *oompah, oompah* all the time."

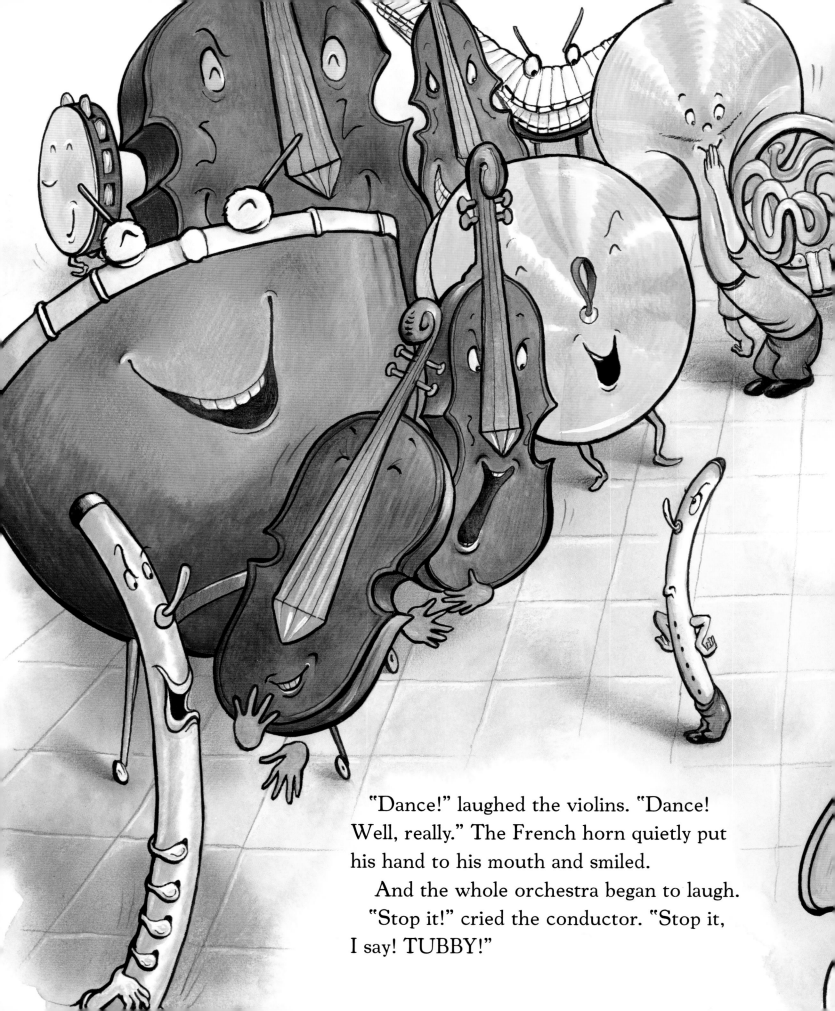

"Dance!" laughed the violins. "Dance! Well, really." The French horn quietly put his hand to his mouth and smiled.

And the whole orchestra began to laugh.

"Stop it!" cried the conductor. "Stop it, I say! TUBBY!"

"Please, sir," said Tubby
sadly, "I wasn't laughing."

Rehearsal was over. Tubby was walking home with Peepo the Piccolo.

"Please, Peepo," said Tubby, "I just feel so bad, I don't think I want any company."

"I understand," said Peepo. "Good night."

"Good night," said Tubby.

The moon was out. Tubby went to the river and sat down on a log. He looked at himself in the water, and he began to sing.

Alone am I.
Me and I together.
If I went away from me,
How unhappy I would be.
Me and I, oh my . . . sigh.

The trees whispered in the wind. The waterfalls tinkled, and an old hoot owl hooted.

Suddenly, a big bullfrog hopped out of the water and sat down beside Tubby.

"Ahem," coughed the frog. "*Bug-Gup! Bug-Gup!* Lovely evening! *Bug-Gup!* I said, *bee-oo-ti-ful* evening. Hello! *Bug-Gup!* Hello! *Bug-Gup!* Hello!"

But Tubby just sat.

"Oh well," said the frog. "Oh well, if I'm not wanted." And he jumped back into the water.

"Oh," cried Tubby, "please, Mr. Frog, come back. I didn't mean to be impolite."

Back hopped the frog.

"Oh, that's all right," said the frog, "I'm used to it. No one pays any attention to me, either."

"Really?" said Tubby.

"Why, of course. Every night I sit here and sing my heart out, but does anyone listen to me? No!"

"Can you sing?" asked Tubby.

"Can I sing?" asked the frog. "Listen!"

The frog started to sing a most
beautiful melody.

"Oh, that's lovely," said Tubby.

"You try it," said the frog.

"Oh, thank you," said Tubby,
and he began to play.

"Say, you're a very fine tuba," said the frog. "Tubby, you should try that melody with your orchestra sometime."

"Oh, I will," said Tubby. "Good-bye, Mr. Frog."

And off went Tubby, as happy as happy could be.

"Hmmm," said the frog, "most appreciative audience I've ever had. Fine musician, that tuba. *Bug-Gup! Bug-Gup!* Lovely evening! *Bug-Gup! Bug-Gup!* . . . Good night."

The next day, the orchestra was busy tuning up for the rehearsal and buzzing with excitement over the arrival of the great new conductor, Signor Pizzicato.

Tubby practiced his *oompah* and smiled to himself.

Peepo the Piccolo caught his eye. "Feeling better?"

"Ah-hah," winked Tubby.

"Here he comes!" called the French horn. "Here comes Signor Pizzicato!"

Signor Pizzicato bowed to the orchestra and raised his baton.

"All right," he said. "Begin!"

And Tubby began to play his own little melody.

"Oh, that wretched tuba!" snapped the violins. "He'll disgrace us!" The trombone stuck out his tongue. And the trumpets snickered.

"Tubby," said Signor Pizzicato. "Tubby, I've never heard a tuba play a melody before. Let's hear the rest of it."

"Oh," said Tubby. "Here's my chance."
And he played with all his heart.

"Why, how perfectly wonderful," murmured the strings. "Please, Tubby, may we sing your tune, too?"

"How about me?" cried the xylophone.

"And me?" said the trombone.

"May I?" said the celeste.
"Here I come!" called Peepo.
And they all played Tubby's melody.

"Well, we've done it, haven't we, Tubby?"

It was the bullfrog, sitting right beside him. "We have our points, too, don't we?"

And—*Oh,* thought Tubby . . .

. . . *how happy I am.*